Albatross, the Survivor

By Jo Windsor

Contents

Albatross, the Survivor	2
How albatrosses fly for long distances	4
How albatrosses catch and store their food	10
How albatross chicks survive	20

Rigby

Albatross, the Survivor

The wandering albatrosses are big sea birds that have two special things that help them survive.

They can fly for long distances without using much energy, and they are able to catch and store food in their bodies for long periods of time. Because of this, these birds can successfully live and breed in a cold environment.

Question:

How do you think albatrosses are able to fly for long distances without using much energy?

?

... without using much energy

How albatrosses fly for long distances

Predict:

What do you think you might find out about in this chapter?

These large and powerful birds are perfectly adapted to live in blustery conditions. They have a flying technique that allows them to fly for long distances without using much energy, or having to come back to land.

They can fly for long periods of time without flapping their wings, using the wind to keep them moving through the air.

All albatrosses fly this way.

Albatrosses can fly for a long time without flapping their wings.

clarify: blustery

A cold
B stormy/windy
C wet

a, b, or c?

Albatrosses can fly for long distances without using much energy.

An albatross needs a lot of wind to keep flying. It can flap its wings, but for much of its flying, an albatross uses the ocean winds to glide.

Wind on the surface of the water moves more slowly than the wind higher up in the air. An albatross uses the slower wind to help it glide. This allows the bird to fly long distances without having to flap its wings.

.... it uses the ocean winds to glide

Question:

Why do you think the wind that is on the surface of the water moves more slowly than the wind higher up?

An albatross begins to glide by making a dive with its wings held in an "m" shape. When it wants to fly higher, it uses the wind coming off the sea to give it lift. To change direction, the albatross shifts the angle of its wings. This type of flying is called dynamic flying. It allows the bird to glide for long periods, conserving its energy.

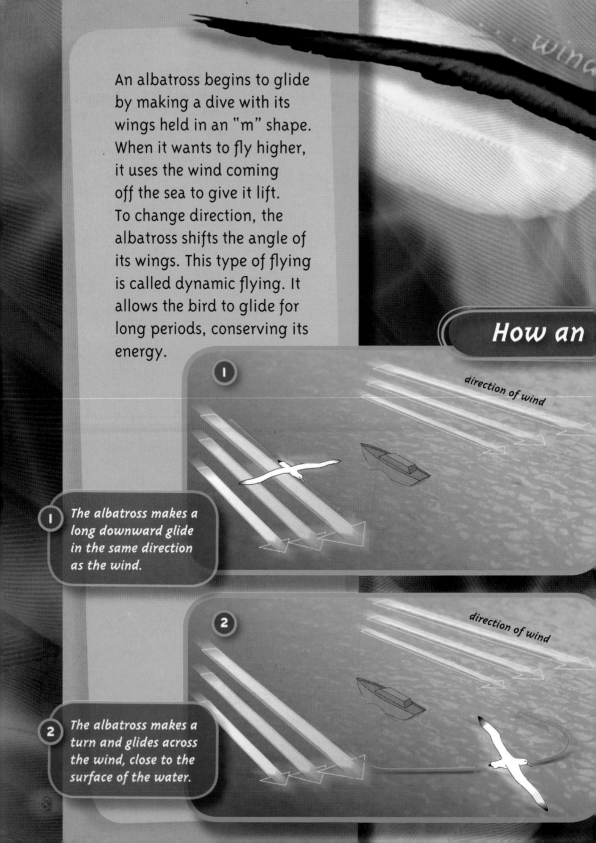

1

direction of wind

1 The albatross makes a long downward glide in the same direction as the wind.

2

direction of wind

2 The albatross makes a turn and glides across the wind, close to the surface of the water.

albatross flies

3

direction of wind

3 The albatross turns again, still close to the surface of the water. It glides into the wind, which slows it down.

4

direction of wind

4 As the albatross begins to lose speed, it turns and makes a steep climb across the wind. It then glides downwind again.

How albatrosses catch and store their food

Predict:

What do you think you might find out about in this chapter?

For most bird species, not having regular food would cause starvation. But, this doesn't happen to an albatross. These birds have a special food-storing tool. Their digestive system can separate food into different weights.

Question generate:

What questions could you ask about this information?

... an albatross feeding frenzy

Albatrosses mostly eat fish and squid. They are also scavengers, and feed on carrion that is floating on the surface of the water.

Sometimes there is a lot of food, but often there is not. Albatrosses sometimes have to travel long distances to find it.

clarify: carrion

A   decaying flesh

B   sea creatures

C   bubbles

a, b, or c?

Albatrosses are scavengers, and feed on carrion.

A feeding albatross grabs its food and swallows it. The food goes into a special chamber. In this chamber, the food is separated into food that will dissolve in water, and food that will not dissolve in water.

The food that will not dissolve in water is made up mostly of oil. This oily food is not as heavy as the watery food, and it floats to the top. The watery food is let out at the bottom of the chamber, just like a separatory funnel.

Question:

What do you think a separatory funnel is?

?

special chamber

oily food layer

watery food layer

Albatrosses have a special chamber that separates the food they eat.

In this diagram you can see how a separatory funnel works.

1 First we pour a mixture of oil (colored yellow) and water (colored blue) into a separatory funnel.

2 The oil and water mix together, but after a while, the oil begins to float to the top of the water.

3 The oil and water separate into two layers.

4 When the hole at the bottom of the funnel is opened, the water will drain out, leaving just the oil.

1 A heavier liquid (blue water) is poured in with a lighter liquid (yellow oil).

A Separatory Funnel

(2) The oil and water mix together.

(3) After a while the lighter liquid (oil) floats to the top.

(4) The water can be let out by opening a hole at the bottom of the funnel.

Cause and Effect

CAUSE	EFFECT
Oil and water are mixed together	?

The albatross continues to catch more food, going through the process of digestion, separation, and draining, until it has stored a large amount of fat that it can take back to its nesting site.

Question:

Why do you think albatrosses need to have large amounts of fat stored in their bodies?

... a large amount of fat

How albatross chicks survive

Predict:

What do you think you might find out about in this chapter?

Parent albatrosses can spend many days or weeks at sea feeding.

When an albatross chick hatches, the parents take turns looking after it. When the chick is older, the parents go off to sea to hunt for food. The chick stays in the nest to sit out the worst of the weather. Usually the parents return to feed the chick about once every three days.

. . . once every three days

The parents take turns sitting on the nest.

Thousands of birds return to the nesting colonies.

Albatrosses usually lay a single egg.

A parent bird passes food to its chick by regurgitation.

The parent birds eat the food they catch, and only partly digest it. When feeding the chick, they bring the partly digested food up out of their stomach and give it to the chick. The chick eats this mixture.

Inference.

What inferences can be made about the digestive system of the chicks?

?

partly digested food

A parent albatross passes food to its chick by regurgitation.

An albatross chick is able to survive on its own for a long time without any extra food. Just like its parents, it can survive on separated food stored in its own stomach.

The fat in the separated food has a lot of energy. Each day, the chick uses up some of the fat.

The young chick can stay in the nest for many days or weeks using its own food.

Question generate:

What questions could you ask about this information?

An albatross chick is able to survive on its own for a long time.

Sometimes the parents do not get back because of bad storms, and the chick is left alone for weeks. During this time, the chick keeps on building up its nest until it is sitting on a high mound of earth and grass. Even on top of this tall nest, a chick can be completely buried if there is a heavy snowfall.

Question:

If you had to make up a glossary for this book, how might you do it and what might you have in it?

The chick keeps on building up its nest.

earth and grass

how albatrosses survive

digesting food 10, 14, 18

getting food 12, 18

storing food 2, 10, 18

using flying techniques 2, 4, 6, 8

how albatross chicks survive

digesting food 22

getting food 20, 22

in the nest 20, 24, 26

storing food 24

Index

Think about the Text

Making connections — What connections can you make to the survival skills explored in *Albatross, the Survivor?*

adapting
to change

traveling long
distances

being
cooperative

Text-
to-Self

caring for
others

learning
to survive

working together

Text-to-Text

Talk about other informational
texts you may have read
that have similar features.
Compare the texts.

Text-to-World

Talk about situations
in the world that connect
to elements in the text.

Planning an Informational Explanation

1. Select a topic that explains why something is the way it is or how something works.

2. Make a mind map of questions about the topic, e.g.

How do albatrosses fly? ← **Albatross, the Survivor** → How do albatrosses survive?

How do albatross chicks survive? ← **Albatross, the Survivor** → What do albatrosses eat?

3. Locate the information that you need.

Library   Internet   Experts

4. Organize your information using the questions you selected as headings.

5 **Make a plan:**

Introduction

The wandering albatrosses
are big sea birds that have
two special tools that help
them survive.

Points in a coherent and logical sequence

How albatrosses fly for long distances	How albatrosses catch and store their food	How albatross chicks survive

6 **Design some visuals to include in your explanation. You can use graphs, diagrams, labels, charts, tables, cross-sections . . .**

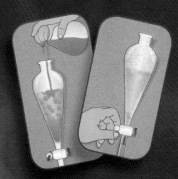

An Informational Explanation . . .

A Explores causes and effects

B Uses scientific and technical vocabulary

C Uses the present tense

D Is written in a formal style that is concise and accurate

E Avoids author opinion